"A rabbit needs space for flopping around
and dreaming of crunchy carrots."

"I know!

I'll go and see Owl.

He's wonderfully wise..."

The Rabbit's Tale

Retold by Lesley Sims

Illustrated by Fred Blunt

"My home is too small," sighed Rabbit, one day.
"I'm feeling all **squished** in."

"Tu-whit, tu-whoo.
What's the matter
with you?"

"My home is too
small. Please can
you help?"

Owl raised his eyes
to the sky.

"I've got it!" he cried, with a flap of his wings.
"Ask all your brothers and sisters to stay."

"Are you sure?" Rabbit said.

"I have quite a few..."

But off he hopped, up hills
and through fields, to ask
his family over.

They poured through the door,
with squeaks and with squeals...

...and munched through his carrots and cake.

"Oh dear!" Rabbit thought. "This won't do at all.
I can't even twitch my whiskers."

Rabbit raced
back to Owl.

"Tu-whit, tu-whoo.
What's the matter with you?"

"I'm even more squashed
than before!"

"Dear me," said Owl, and thought for a while.
"Try asking your friends over too."

"How can that work?
Well, I'll give it
a whirl."

"Hello
Tortoise."

"Hello Mole."

"Please come to my
house for cake."

With a leap and a scamper, everyone came
and **squeezed** into Rabbit's house.

"Help!" thought Rabbit. "This can't be right.
I can hardly breathe."

He dashed back to Owl.

"Now there's NO room for me!"

"Then it's time for them all to leave."

Rabbit waved goodbye
as they left one by one.

"Bye, bye!"

"How's your house now, Rabbit?"

Edited by Jenny Tyler and Susanna Davidson
Digital manipulation by Nick Wakeford
Designed by Caroline Spatz

First published in 2013 by Usborne Publishing Ltd., Usborne House, 83-85 Saffron Hill, London EC1N 8RT, England.
www.usborne.com
Copyright © 2013 Usborne Publishing Ltd.